Michael Hall

Wonderfall

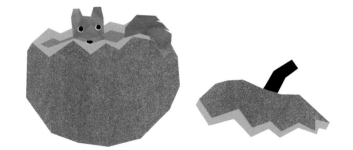

GREENWILLOW BOOKS
An Imprint of HarperCollinsPublishers

Wonderfall

Copyright © 2016 by Michael Hall

All rights reserved.
Manufactured in China.

For information address
HarperCollins Children's Books,
a division of HarperCollins Publishers,
195 Broadway, New York, NY 10007.
www.harpercollinschildrens.com

The digitally rendered images incorporate textures
created with acrylic paint and soft pastels.
The text type is 18-point Avenir Light.

Library of Congress Cataloging-in-Publication Data is available.

ISBN 978-0-06-238298-6 (trade ed.)

"Greenwillow Books."

16 17 18 19 20 SCP 10 9 8 7 6 5 4 3 2 1

First Edition

Greenwillow Books

For

Wendy,

Anne,

Kathy,

and

John

Peacefall

A gentle
breeze is
jiggling
me.

I hear
my
acorns
drop.

Plink,
plunk,
plop.

Dutifall

Beep!

The busy
yellow
bus is
back.

I haven't
seen it
since
last
spring.

Plentifall

Apples,
apples,
ready to
munch.

Yellow,
red,
green—
*crunch,
crunch!*

Beautifall

Autumn
colors,
all around.

And look
(*rustle, rustle*)—
I'm dressed
for the
season,
too.

Eventfall

I've got
the spot
for this
parade.
*Tat boom,
tat boom,
tat boom!*

Frightfall

Howling
cats and
fluttering
bats.
Welcome,
ghosts
and goblins.
Tonight
the streets
belong
to you. . . .

Boo!

Thankfall

Gather
together.
*Gobble,
gobble.*
*Yum,
yum.*

Delightfall

What's
this?
Oh, my!

My
friends
found
a piece of
pumpkin
pie.

Playfall

Look

who's

chasing

in my

branches.

Look

who's

romping

in my

leaves.

Forcefall

Whoosh,
whoosh,
whoa!

What
wild,
whirling
wind!

Helpfall

Hooray,
hooray!
The
cleanup
crew
arrived
today.

Resourcefall

Chopped,
bagged,
stomped,
and stowed,
my leaves
will make
marvelous
mulch.

Wistfall

Good-bye,
geese.

I'm sad
to see
you go.

Watchfall

See

the mist.

Hear

the quiet.

Smell

the cold.

Will

this night . . .

bring

the

first . . .

snowfall!

Getting ready for winter

Fall is here! I'm showing off my colors. What is everyone else doing?

When an animal **hibernates**, it builds or finds a warm den or roost where it can spend the winter. Hibernating animals store up food and sleep a lot!

When an animal **migrates**, it usually heads south in the fall and returns north in the spring. Some birds and insects fly long distances in order to find food and return to their first nesting grounds.

The **Monarch Butterflies** that are born in late summer and early fall migrate south, to California and Mexico. They can travel for thousands of miles. When winter ends, they start north again.

Little Brown Bats hibernate when it gets cold (sometimes migrating a little to reach good hibernating areas). But when the weather warms up, even on a winter day, they will leave the roost to hunt for food.

Cardinals and Indigo Buntings are songbirds. Indigo buntings migrate at night, following the stars. Cardinals stay put during the winter.

Some **Canada Geese** migrate, but others—who have discovered good things to eat in neighborhoods with open water—stay right where they are through the winter. Geese travel with their families, flying in V-shaped flocks through the air.

Snowshoe Hares change color with the seasons. In the winter their coats are white and in the spring, brown. They are fast and shy, and they mostly come out at night.

White-tailed Deer live in herds, or groups. In the fall, the male deer shows off the beautiful antlers he has been growing all year. In winter, they sometimes stand on their back legs to reach a tasty leaf or paw through the snow to find an acorn.

Raccoons are most active at night. They eat as much as possible in the fall so that they have enough fat and energy for the cold winter months. Raccoons live together in small dens in tree trunks or woodpiles or old sheds.

Great Horned Owls nest in stumps and old trees and hunt during the night, so they are hard to spot. But you can hear them! Most great horned owls do not migrate or hibernate.

Red Foxes live in family groups and can walk for miles in a day. In the fall and winter their coats turn even redder, and their bushy tails keep them warm in their dens.

Gray squirrels and acorns

Plink, plunk, plop!
In autumn,
my acorns drop.
What happens next?

Gray squirrels eat my tasty acorns. Squirrels are sensible animals. They store thousands of acorns in holes in the ground to make sure they have food for the winter. Squirrels are quite good at digging into the snow to fetch these acorns, but they are better at hiding acorns than they are at finding them. So most of the buried acorns stay in the ground.

Since each acorn contains a seed, the squirrels are actually planting my seeds far and wide.

oak tree seed

acorn shell

I love to watch new saplings sprout up from those seeds in the spring.

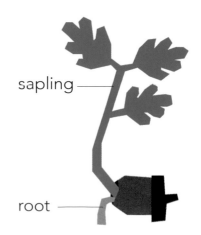

sapling

root

I thank the gray squirrels by being a safe home for them. They can climb up my trunk to escape from a hungry fox. They can hide in my branches to avoid a swooping hawk or owl. And, during the coldest parts of winter, gray squirrels can take shelter in a hole in my trunk. They might stay there, cozy and warm, for several days.

I offer the squirrels my leaves and twigs so they can make nests in my branches. Most often, there is one squirrel to a nest, and most squirrels have several nests to sleep in.

Squirrels are comfortable living near people. They will look for food in trash cans. They will nibble on patio plants. If you happen to leave a mitten on the ground, a squirrel might very well snatch it and build it into its nest.

What about me?

You might be wondering how I get through the winter. I don't have legs or wings, so I can't migrate. I can't make a nest or crawl into a den. Instead, I go into a state that is like a long, deep sleep. It's called **dormancy**. I stop growing and need very little energy.

During the summer months my roots soak up water from the ground and my leaves capture energy from sunlight. But when fall arrives and the days get shorter and colder, I don't need my leaves anymore. I drop them as I prepare for winter. I sleep beneath a blanket of snow until I feel spring in the air.